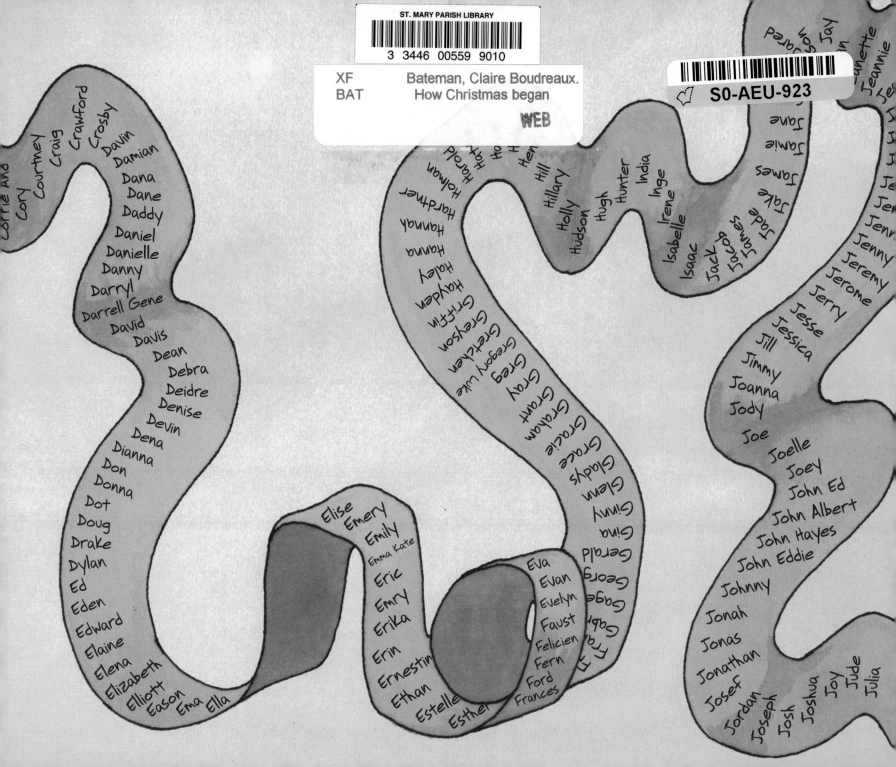

How Christmas Began

Published in the United States 2002 by Shell Beach Publishing

677 Shell Beach Drive, Lake Charles, LA 70601

Illustrations by Hannah Elaine Romero

Designed by Chris Steiner

Digital Photography by David Humphreys

ISBN 0-9706732-1-3

Printed in China

Second Edition

special thanks:

Kay Blake, Renee Bacher, Maggie Richardson, Mary Anne Bertrand, Lisa Henry,

Elena and Kyle Keegan, James Fontenot, John Theriot, Sarah Kracke, Carol Hill, Lorilin Braymer,

Kay Rousseau, Stacey Miremont, Danny Plaisance, Jo Ann Hardeman, John Bennett and Robin Mayhall

If your whole body is full of light, and no part of it

is in darkness, then it will be as full of light as a lamp

illuminating you with its brightness. *Luke 11:36*

To my **whole** family, especially

Drew, David, Mom and Dad for

showing me the special glow of Jesus

A long, long time ago, before there were Christmas presents, Christmas trees or even Christmas dinners, Jesus, who was just a little boy, was playing with his good friend Santa Claus. They were helping each other catch frogs. "Jesus," Santa said, "You're a good friend. How many people in the world have a heart like yours?"

Jesus smiled, "A lot, I think! But let's find out!"

"How do you think we'll know?" asked Santa.

"That will be easy," Jesus said. "They are the ones who are kind and sweet to each other, obey their parents, forgive one another...

...and share with others."

Santa thought for a minute, "Hey Jesus! We could make a list of all those people! Maybe I could fly around the whole wide world and look for them. I could be *invisible!*" Jesus laughed. Then Santa laughed. They laughed and laughed until their bellies hurt. Everyone knows boys can't fly and be invisible.

Then Jesus remembered
He could help Santa.

So He blessed him.

Now Santa really could fly around the world and look for everyone who loved Jesus and had that **special glow** in their hearts.

Santa got busy with his list. He watched and listened
to many, many boys and girls as they played and worked.

He made the **biggest, longest** list of names you ever saw. Jesus was so happy to see all those names that He jumped for joy!

Jesus thought about that big list for a while and then said, "Santa, I have the **greatest idea!** It is almost my birthday and because all of these people have my special glow...each one of them should get a birthday present!"

"That's a great idea, Jesus. Then everyone can celebrate your birthday. It'll be the biggest birthday party in the world!"

Jesus needed help getting presents for all of those special people. He and Santa wanted to be sure no one would find out about their big plans. So up they went to the North Pole, far, far, away from where any people lived.

Jesus built Santa a **great big** house with elves and reindeer and everything he would need to be ready for Jesus' big birthday party.

On the morning of Jesus' birthday, children and grown-ups around the world woke up to the biggest birthday party ever!

There were presents for everyone!

The best present was that people started seeing
that special part of Jesus inside each other's hearts.
They realized that when someone received a present,
that "Christ must" live inside of them. That's where
the word **Christmas** came from.

It was a **huge** success!
Jesus and Santa decided
they should do this
every year.

As time went on, people started decorating trees and having family and friends over for dinner...throwing wonderful parties for Jesus' birthday.

And that is how Christmas, the wonderful celebration
of love, joy and happiness, began.

Julian, Julianna, Julie, Justin, Jutta, K.C. Ann, Kale Ana, Kale, Karen, Kaley, Kassandra, Kathryn, Kathy, Kirby, Katy, Kay, Kayla, Keely, Kelsey, Kermit, Kelly, Kenneth, Kent, Kevin, Kimberly, Kirsten, Korin

Kristen, Kyra, Kyle, Lakin, Lala, Lance, Landice, Lane

Liz, Lilly, Laura, Lauren, Leah Ann, Leila, Leneta, Leslie, Levi, Lexie, Lil' Romeo, Liam Dale, Lilah, Lillian, Lindsey, Linda, Lisa, Lola, Lona, Lori, Lorraine, Lothar, Louis, Louise, Lucas, Lucy, Luke, Lydia, Lynn, Mackie, Macy, Maddie, Madeline, Madeline Mae, Madelyn, Madison, Madisyn, Maggie Jo, Maggie, Mandalyn, Marsha, Malloy, Mandy, Marcus, Marcy, Maria, Martha, Mariel, Marielle, Marien, Marion, Mark, Marque Ann, Marshall, Marty, Mary, Mary, Margaret, Mary Grace, Mary Kate, Maryanne, Matt

Mama, Martin, Matthew, Max, McCraney, McKenzie, Megan, Meghan, Melanie, Melissa, Merry, Mia, Micah, Micheal, Michele, Michelle, Mickey, Montgomery, Mike, Mikey, Miles, Miller, Milton Rex, Mimi, Minya, Miranda, Mischa, Molly, Monica, Morgan, Murphy, Myra, Myrn, Nairn